PINE HILLS BRANCH
ALBANY PUBLIC LIBRARY

S0-BAV-225

This Is My Truck/
Éste es mi camión

By/por Amanda Hudson

Reading Consultant: Susan Nations, M.Ed.,
author/literacy coach/consultant in literacy development/

Consultora de lectura: Susan Nations, M.Ed.,
autora/tutora de alfabetización/consultora de desarrollo de lectoescritura

WEEKLY READER®
PUBLISHING

Please visit our web site at www.garethstevens.com
For a free catalog describing our list of high-quality books,
call 1-800-542-2595 (USA) or 1-800-387-3178 (Canada).
Our fax: 1-877-542-2596

Library of Congress Cataloging-in-Publication Data

Hudson, Amanda.
     (This is my truck. Spanish & English)
     This is my truck = Éste es mi camión / Amanda Hudson.
        p. cm. — (Our toys = Nuestros juguetes)
     ISBN-10: 0-8368-9259-3   ISBN-13: 978-0-8368-9259-8 (lib. bdg.)
     ISBN-10: 0-8368-9358-1   ISBN-13: 978-0-8368-9358-8 (pbk.)
      1. Vocabulary—Juvenile literature. 2. Trucks—Juvenile literature.
  I. Title. II. Title: Éste es mi camión.
PE1449.H7718   2009
428.1—dc22
                                             2008014472

This edition first published in 2009 by
Weekly Reader® Books
An Imprint of Gareth Stevens Publishing
1 Reader's Digest Road
Pleasantville, NY 10570-7000 USA

Copyright © 2009 by Gareth Stevens, Inc.

Senior Managing Editor: Lisa M. Herrington
Creative Director: Lisa Donovan
Electronic Production Manager: Paul Bodley, Jr.
Designer: Alexandria Davis
Cover Designer: Amelia Favazza, *Studio Montage*
Photographer: Richard Hutchings
Translation: Tatiana Acosta and Guillermo Gutiérrez

All rights reserved. No part of this book may be reproduced, stored in a retrieval system, or transmitted in any form or by any means, electronic, mechanical, photocopying, recording, or otherwise, without the prior written permission of the copyright holder.

Printed in the United States of America

1 2 3 4 5 6 7 8 9 10 09 08

Note to Educators and Parents

Learning to read is one of the most exciting and challenging things young children do. Among other skills, they are beginning to match the spoken word to print and learn directionality and print conventions.

The books in the *Our Toys* series are designed to support young readers in the earliest stages of literacy. Children will love looking at the full-color photographs while also being challenged to think about words that name objects and how those words fit into a basic sentence structure.

In addition to serving as wonderful picture books in schools, libraries, and homes, this series is specifically intended to be read within instructional small groups. The small group setting enables the teacher or other adult to provide scaffolding that will boost the reader's efforts. Children and adults alike will find these books supportive, engaging, and fun!

—Susan Nations, M.Ed.,
author, literacy coach, and consultant in literacy development

Nota para los maestros y los padres

Aprender a leer es una de las actividades más emocionantes y estimulantes que realizan los niños pequeños. Entre otras destrezas, a esta edad están comenzando a integrar su manejo del lenguaje oral con el lenguaje escrito, y a aprender las convenciones de la letra impresa y la dirección de la lectura.

Los libros de la colección *Nuestros juguetes* están pensados para ayudar a los jóvenes lectores en las primeras etapas del proceso de lectoescritura. A los niños les gustará mirar las fotografías a todo color y pensar en los nombres de los objetos, y en cómo estas palabras encajan en la estructura básica de una oración.

Además de servir como maravillosos libros ilustrados en escuelas, bibliotecas y hogares, los libros de esta colección han sido especialmente concebidos para ser leídos en grupos de lectura guiada. Este contexto permite que un maestro u otro adulto proporcione la orientación necesaria para estimular el esfuerzo de los lectores. ¡Estos libros les resultarán útiles, estimulantes y divertidos a niños y a adultos por igual!

— Susan Nations, M.Ed.,
autora/tutora de alfabetización/consultora de desarrollo de la lectura

fire truck

camión de bomberos

This is my fire truck.
Éste es mi camión de bomberos.

mail truck
_ _ _ _ _ _
camión del correo

This is my mail truck.
Éste es mi camión del correo.

garbage truck
camión de la basura

This is my garbage truck.
Éste es mi camión de la basura.

9

tow truck
_ _ _ _ _ _
camión grúa

This is my tow truck.
Éste es mi camión grúa.

tanker truck
camión cisterna

This is my tanker truck.
Éste es mi camión cisterna.

dump truck

camión de volteo

This is my dump truck.
Éste es mi camión de volteo.

This is not a truck!

¡Esto no es un camión!